To all the dogs all the world over—and the people who love them.

www.mascotbooks.com

Judah's Promise

For more information, please contact:
Mascot Books
560 Herndon Parkway #120
Herndon, VA 20170
info@mascotbooks.com

Library of Congress Control Number: 2016915223

CPSIA Code: PRT0317A
ISBN-13: 978-1-63177-393-8

Printed in the United States

Judah's Promise

Written by
Irene Maslowski

Illustrated by
Laurie Barrows

Adam felt sad. His best friend, a boxer dog named Judah, recently passed away.

Sitting up in bed, Adam looked out the window. *I miss you so much, Judah. I worry about you and wonder where you are, and I wish I could see you one more time.*

While Adam was sleeping, a dog floated down from the sky and into Adam's room.

"But you can see me again," he whispered. "I'm here now."

"Judah, is that you?"

"Yes, it's me," Judah replied.

"But how can that be, how did you get here?"

"I flew down on the wings of a special friend from a special place way beyond the sky, the stars, and the planets," said Judah.

"It's called World's End and I've come to take you there for a visit so you can see that I am okay."

Judah brought Adam to the window.

"Hello, Adam. So nice to meet you," said a fairy. "I am Lady Allison."

"The visit is just for a little while and then we'll bring you back in time for morning," said Judah.

"How can you do that?"
asked Adam.

"Lady Allison has flying
powers and special
pillows in her wings where
we can sit together.
We'll sail into the night
and take you on a great
adventure," Judah said.

"Climb aboard!" she
exclaimed.

They flew for a short while and soon something appeared on the horizon.

It looked like a little island right in the middle of the sky, with trees and flowers and sparkling sunshine.

"Where is this place?" Adam asked.

"This is World's End. It's where I live now," Judah replied. "It's where all dogs and cats come to live when they can no longer stay on Earth. It's called World's End because it is just on the edge of Earth where we can still see our loved ones and watch them every day."

They entered the gates of World's End and Adam saw dogs and cats running, playing games, and frolicking about.

"Come with me," said Judah. "I'll show you around."

Adam, Judah, and Lady Allison soon came to a lake.

"Here's where we swim," said Judah. "And here's our picnic area. When we get tired of playing, here's where we take a nap."

"We play lots of games too, just like we did on Earth," said Judah. "Dogs chasing cats and cats chasing dogs."

"There's our neighbor Mrs. Lopez's cat, Dolce!" exclaimed Adam. "And I see Grandma's dog, Ginger!"

"Yes," Judah said. "We are all here, safe and sound and having a good time. Would you like to join them and have some fun?"

"Yes!" Adam answered excitedly.

They joined the other cats and dogs at the lake. "Come on, Adam. Let's go for a boat ride with Judah and Dolce and have a picnic," said Ginger.

"It's getting late," said Judah, looking at the sun. When the sun goes down here, it comes up back home. It's time for me to get you back for school."

"Bye, Ginger. Bye, Dolce," said Adam.

"Goodbye, Adam," they replied.

Judah and Lady Allison helped get Adam home.

"I will miss you, Judah," cried Adam.

"I'm always with you. I think of you as much as you think of me, and I will come back to you someday soon for another visit."

"How can I make sure that happens?" Adam cried.

"You must believe with all your heart that someday we will see those we love again, even though they are no longer part of this world. "Judah replied. "As long as you believe that, all things are possible. I promise I will come to you again."

Judah

ABOUT THE AUTHOR

Irene Maslowski is a debut children's author and a public relations professional in New Jersey. She is passionate about reading, literacy, and animals.

The loss of a beloved pet can be difficult for adults, but it can be devastating for children, particularly those who have not experienced loss or have not yet developed the necessary coping skills to help them deal with their grief.

This book was written to help youngsters understand the emotions that we all feel when we lose a pet we love, and that it's okay to believe that someday we may have a chance to be with them again.

Have a book idea?
Contact us at:

info@mascotbooks.com | www.mascotbooks.com